THE SECRET KNOWLEDGE OF GROWN-UPS

TOP SECRET

CLASSIFIED
SECURITY
CLEARANCE

The Second File

For Ariana and Alexander

The Secret Knowledge of Grown-ups: The Second File
Copyright (c) 2001 by David Wisniewski
Printed in the U.S.A. All rights reserved.
www.harperchildrens.com

Library of Congress Cataloging-in-Publication Data
Wisniewski, David.
The secret knowledge of grown-ups: the second file/revealed and
illustrated by David Wisniewski.
p.   cm.
ISBN 0-688-17854-5—ISBN 0-688-17855-3 (lib. bdg.)
1. Children—Juvenile humor.   2. Adulthood—Juvenile humor.
[1. Behavior—Wit and humor.   2. Parent and child—Wit and humor.]   I. Title.
PN6231.C32 W58   2001   CIP
818'.5402—dc21   00-049875
AC

1 2 3 4 5 6 7 8 9 10
❖
First Edition

You now hold The Second File of The Secret Knowledge of Grown-ups. Open it, and you will find the mind-boggling truth--the stark, raving reality--behind all these supposedly harmless pleas! It took countless hours to compile and verify--sneaking through complex security systems, clad in foolproof disguises, seizing the most guarded secrets of adulthood.

But hurry! You haven't much time!

WAIT! Did you hear that? Was that the creak of a door? A step on the stairs? THEY'RE COMING! I must go!

Quickly! Read this book!

LEARN MORE OF THE TRUTH!

LOCATION:
McCullen Shoe Factory
Wattakonk, Massachusetts

DATE & TIME:
February 1, 2000
11:30 P.M.

LOG: Sneak in as sneaker. Boot up computer as boot. Download *GROWN-UP RULE #12*! Suddenly tried on by night watchman! Transform to high heel. Cause embarrassing fashion statement. Slip away as slipper.

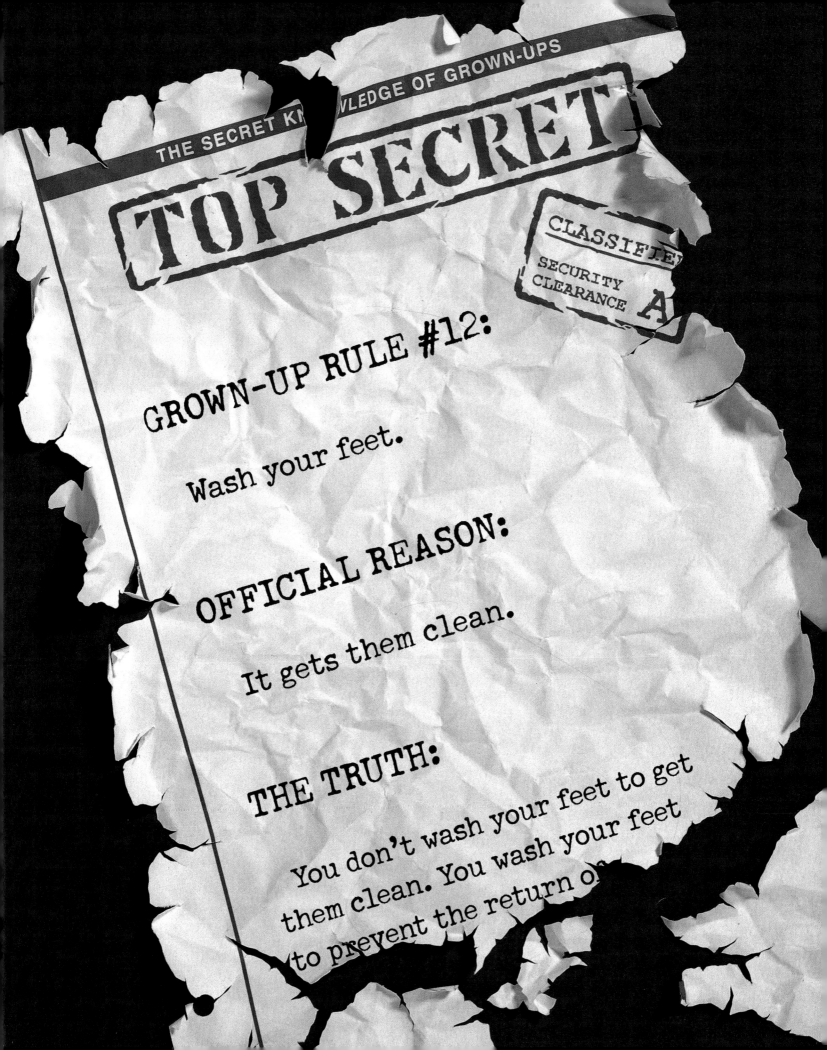

THE SECRET KNOWLEDGE OF GROWN-UPS

TOP SECRET

CLASSIFIED
SECURITY
CLEARANCE A

GROWN-UP RULE #12:

Wash your feet.

OFFICIAL REASON:

It gets them clean.

THE TRUTH:

You don't wash your feet to get them clean. You wash your feet to prevent the return of

Early American foot farms!

After the *Mayflower* hit Plymouth Rock and sank, the Pilgrims swam to the forbidding shores of Massachusetts. Doffing their saturated shoes and socks, the newcomers trudged through the loamy soil in search of roots, nuts, and shopping malls. Finding only snack machines filled with pemmican,* they marched back to their abandoned footwear. Along the way the Pilgrims' wet feet picked up more layers of fertile earth.

*pemmican: cakes of fat flavored with meat and berries. From the Cree Indian word *pimikew*, meaning "he who makes grease." Scholars think this stuff is the ancestor of today's Double Whopper with Cheese.

Meantime, their shoes and socks were stolen by three bears waiting for their porridge to cool. Pinched by hunger and shrinking underwear, the Pilgrims bemoaned their fate.

They were heard by a Wampanoag Indian named Squanto, meaning "he who squants." Moved by their plight and amused by their funny hats, he taught the Pilgrims how to plant seeds in their dirt-laden tootsies. In a few months the newcomers were shuffling around with impressive crops of corn, pumpkins, and beans.

Squanto also showed the Pilgrims how to fertilize their foot farms with pulverized fish. This resulted in greater harvests and fewer dates. It also caused Squanto to run into the woods and laugh himself sick.

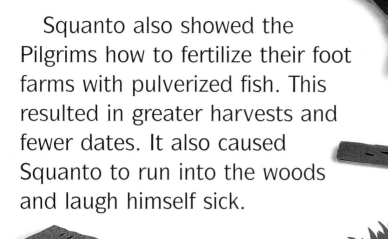

Ye Tragical Deathe of Brewster Scrooby

showed the necessity of weeding Early American foot farms. While poking a hoe into his tangle of creepers and vines, Scrooby disturbed a hibernating bear.

The Pilgrim ran away, but the annoyed animal remained directly in front of him. It ended badly.

As the poem cautions:

Weede thy Feete
Both Here and There,
Lest thou be eaten by a Beare.
Hoe thy Toes
And keepe them neate,
Lest thou find Critters in thy Feete.

In time planting seeds in actual ground replaced the Early American foot farm. The Pilgrims greeted this innovation gladly. They wore shoes again. They started smelling better than an aquarium. The women began wearing makeup from the Mayflower Compact.

EFFECTS OF MAYFLOWER COMPACT

BEFORE | AFTER

The Pilgrims celebrated by inviting Squanto and his tribe to a meal with duck, goose, deer, and shellfish. Everyone was very thankful, mainly because Squanto had forgotten to bring pemmican. Thus began National Cholesterol Awareness Day!

So wash your feet! "Yeah, right!" you may reply. "A foot full of barley doesn't happen overnight."

Perhaps . . . but feet get corns pretty quickly. And wash behind your ears while you're at it—unless you really like potatoes!

LOCATION:
National Dental Association
Washington, D.C.

DATE & TIME: March 21, 2000
2:15 A.M.

LOG: Enter premises as Tooth Fairy. Costume works! Guards hand over dentures, hoping for big payoff. While writing checks, discover *GROWN-UP RULE #23* on reception desk! Rope snaps! Bruise wand. Break tutu.

THE SECRET KNOWLEDGE OF GROWN-UPS

TOP SECRET

CLASSIFIED

SECURITY CLEARANCE **A**

GROWN-UP RULE #23:

Brush your teeth.

OFFICIAL REASON:

It prevents cavities.

THE TRUTH:

Yes, brushing your teeth prevents cavities, but it's hardly the real reason.

You brush your teeth

You have to remember: Being a tooth isn't a great job. Most teeth would rather be doing something else. Read this troubling X ray of Moe Larr, a disgruntled bicuspid residing at #3 Lower Right Jaw, Inside Travis Dibble's Head, Bunce, Minnesota.

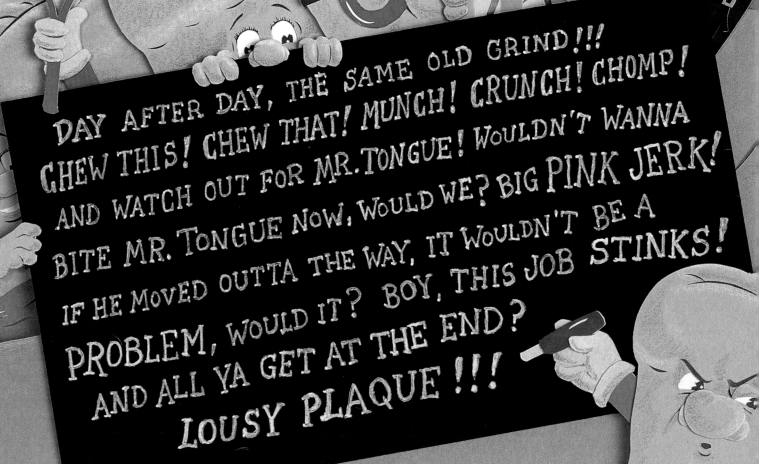

DAY AFTER DAY, THE SAME OLD GRIND!!! CHEW THIS! CHEW THAT! MUNCH! CRUNCH! CHOMP! AND WATCH OUT FOR MR. TONGUE! WOULDN'T WANNA BITE MR. TONGUE NOW, WOULD WE? BIG PINK JERK! IF HE MOVED OUTTA THE WAY, IT WOULDN'T BE A PROBLEM, WOULD IT? BOY, THIS JOB STINKS! AND ALL YA GET AT THE END? LOUSY PLAQUE!!!

Without brushing, teeth rebel against their boring lives. They throw wild parties and dance to loud, obnoxious music.

Reckless incisors cavort with wanton tooth wrecker Ginger Vitus as heartbroken gum looks on.

Such careless behavior can lead to permanent separation between tooth and gum.

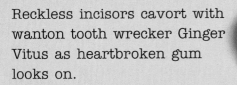

Pulp rocker Tommy Rot sings inflammatory lyrics to a frenzied crowd:

"These roots were made for walkin', and that's just what they'll do! And one of these days, these roots are gonna walk all over you!"

Unless brushing resumes, disorder grows. Fights break out, engulfing whole neighborhoods!

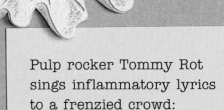

The worst incident was the Galveston Tooth Riot of 1872. Thousands of rootin', tootin' Texas teeth brawled in the streets. After three days of chaos, the federal government sent in Tactical Assault Dentists (TADs) to restore order. Five weeks of brutal mouth-to-mouth fighting ensued.

Dr. Morris Q. Rinsenspitt, last surviving TAD of the Galveston Tooth Riot, astride his valiant horse, Malocclusion. "I got thar kinda late," the nearsighted dentist admitted, "on account of because mah horse didn't have no head."

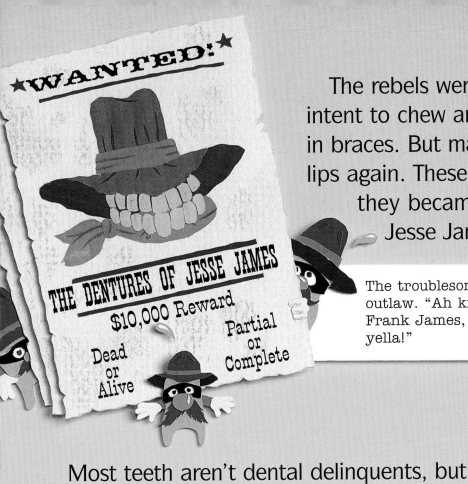

The rebels were found guilty of assault with intent to chew and sent back to their owners in braces. But many couldn't face life behind lips again. These teeth fled to Missouri, where they became the dentures of outlaw Jesse James.

The troublesome teeth eventually deserted the outlaw. "Ah knew them teeth was cowards," stated Frank James, the bandit's brother. "They was yella!"

Most teeth aren't dental delinquents, but they do want a break or a brief vacation. Dentists prevent this by checking your teeth with a little mirror. People think they're looking for cavities. Nope! They're searching for suitcases, coolers, and beach umbrellas—telltale signs of teeth getting ready to travel.

It's also why dentists use a scraper. "You have tartar buildup back here," they say. Baloney! They're digging out some poor tooth's bowling ball or set of skis.

In conclusion, control your teeth with regular brushing. They feel that toothbrush and say, "Darn! He knows we're in here. Cancel that flight to Bermuda!"

LOCATION: Miss Meryl's Maid Service
Frammis, Indiana

DATE & TIME: June 2, 2000
8:45 P.M.

LOG: Clean way into dispatch office camouflaged as feather duster. Find *GROWN-UP RULE #32* in service schedule! Approached by Miss Meryl's pet parrot. Rather than cause incident, go out for dinner and movie. Says I remind him of his mother. Loser!

TOP SECRET

CLASSIFIED

SECURITY CLEARANCE A

GROWN-UP RULE #32:

Clean under your bed.

OFFICIAL REASON:

It keeps it tidy.

THE TRUTH:

Well, duh! But why bother if nobody ever looks there? The real reason is to stop the horrific growth of

killer dust bunnies!

Yes, it's true! Dust bunnies aren't just swirling clumps of dirty fluff. They're *living* clumps of dirty fluff!

"So what?" you may say. "They're under the bed. I sleep on top!"

Just this: Dust bunnies can easily combine to form larger, more dangerous dust animals. For instance, Chinese dust bunnies turn into dust pandas, while Australian dust bunnies become dust kangaroos. Scientists think this has to do with the type of dust in a certain area. This hypothesis was proven the hard way by the intrepid Dr. Harold Wilberforce in a disastrous series of dust bunny expeditions.

THE FIRST WILBERFORCE EXPEDITION (1948)

While sweeping under beds in rural India, scientists were surprised by dust cobras. Without thinking, they hid under another bed, where they were eaten by ferocious dust tigers. Dr. Wilberforce was the sole survivor.

THE SECOND WILBERFORCE EXPEDITION (1949)

As the team cleaned under beds in an Alaskan igloo, they were caught off guard by dust polar bears. The terrified scientists escaped but perished in the frozen wilderness. They are still used by the local people as doorstops. Again, only Dr. Wilberforce survived.

THE THIRD WILBERFORCE EXPEDITION (1950)

Thinking he would be safe from dust animals if he stayed away from beds, Dr. Wilberforce ran his Amazon River expedition from a cast iron bathtub. Unfortunately he was eaten by dust piranhas the first night out.

As you can see, cleaning under your bed is a good idea. If you haven't done it for a while, though, send your brother or sister in ahead of you. In the meantime, be on the lookout for any signs of dust bunny evolution. The last thing we need is a bunch of short dirty kids named Fluffy Clumps.

LOCATION:
Kramer Vending Products, Inc.
Arbogast, North Carolina

DATE & TIME: November 30, 2000
8:30 A.M.

LOG: Enter warehouse
concealed inside vending
machine. Locate *GROWN-UP
RULE #47* on inventory list!
Machine suddenly shipped to
ice rink. Hockey team annoyed
by lack of snacks. Must get
puck removed.

TOP SECRET

CLASSIFIED

SECURITY CLEARANCE A

GROWN-UP RULE #47:

Don't eat junk food.

OFFICIAL REASON:

It's bad for you.

THE TRUTH:

Sure, junk food is bad for you, but in a far more serious way than ___ think. Parents don't want you t___ ecome a path___tic vict___m of

brainjacking!

What?! *Incredible!* Malnutritionists from the infamous Bureau Against Real Food have blocked your view of this snack-induced malady! Will these high-calorie crooks stop at nothing to conceal the truth? Quickly! On to the science behind this dreadful condition!

By eating snack machines full of junk food, scientists discovered they should have gotten the food out of the machines first. They also found the four Cruddy Food Groups: sugar, salt, fat, and grease. These Cruddy Food Groups (CFGs) are different from the Basic Food Groups (BFGs).

Nutrition pioneer Norman "Knobs" Fetterman after eating a vending machine full of junk food in 1948. He reported no ill effects except for an embarrassing ability to make change when a dollar bill was put in his mouth.

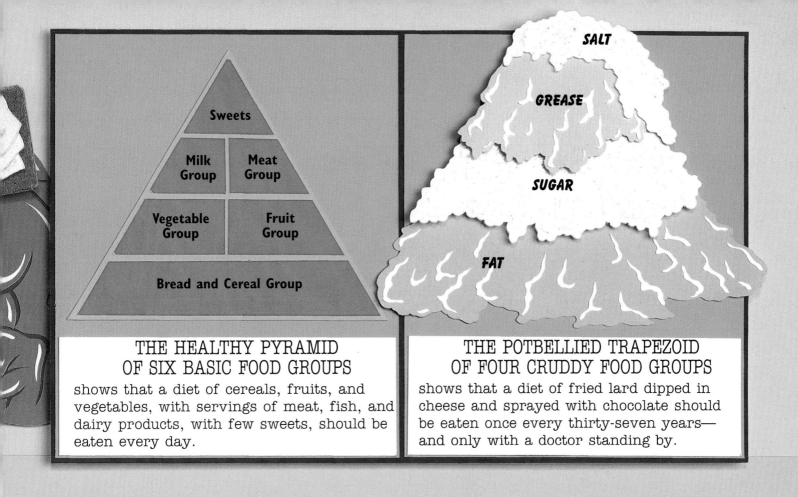

THE HEALTHY PYRAMID
OF SIX BASIC FOOD GROUPS

shows that a diet of cereals, fruits, and vegetables, with servings of meat, fish, and dairy products, with few sweets, should be eaten every day.

THE POTBELLIED TRAPEZOID
OF FOUR CRUDDY FOOD GROUPS

shows that a diet of fried lard dipped in cheese and sprayed with chocolate should be eaten once every thirty-seven years—and only with a doctor standing by.

Simply put, CFGs are bad for you. Sugar decays teeth. Salt raises blood pressure. Fat causes you to leave potholes instead of footprints. Grease makes your lips slide off. These effects are disturbing, but they can be reversed. *Brainjacking cannot!*

Here's what happens: When a double cheeseburger, large fries, and soda land in your stomach, CFG molecules are released into your bloodstream. Wearing cheap suits and dark glasses, they take cabs to a rundown hotel outside your brain. Without tipping, they enter the room, pull the shades, and wait.

Once you're asleep, they break into your brain! Each molecule steals a tiny bit and drives it to an abandoned warehouse in an unpleasant industrial section of your body. The brain cell is blindfolded and tied to a chair while the CFG molecule laughs evilly and rubs its hands together.

Incredibly, upon waking, you never notice this has happened. Although your brain is now held hostage in millions of places around your body, it still functions normally.

"Well, then," you might say, "what's the big deal?"

The big deal happens when you grow up. After years of junk food, your doctor will recommend diet and exercise to lose weight. But with your brain spread around, *you can't lose weight without losing intelligence!*

You'll have a tough choice:
1. Stay fat and smart.
2. Become thin and dumb.

Believe me, it's easier to defeat brainjacking CFGs while you're a kid. Eat foods from the Basic Food Groups. It doesn't take much—a piece of celery or glass of milk will do.

Immediately, BFG molecules race to the rescue in police cars. They kick down the doors and wrestle the CFG molecules to the ground. The brain cells are freed to reassemble into the usual human brain.

To stop the scourge of brainjacking, stay away from junk food. And work more iron into your diet too. Then the BFG molecules can build a few prisons to keep those bad boys from causing trouble.

LOCATION:
Poseidon Plumbing Supply
Lower Tooting, Delaware

DATE & TIME: January 5, 2001
11:00 P.M.

LOG: Thanks to industrial-strength girdle, access facility as mop. Snatch *GROWN-UP RULE #51* from file room! Abruptly grabbed by janitor. Feet stuffed in bucket! Wrung through wringer! Girdle explodes. Rocket to safety.

THE SECRET KNOWLEDGE OF GROWN-UPS

TOP SECRET

CLASSIFIED

SECURITY CLEARANCE A

GROWN-UP RULE #51:

Don't stay in the bathtub too long.

OFFICIAL REASON:

You'll get cold.

THE TRUTH:

Sure, bathwater gets cold. But that's not the reason parents demand limited tub time. The real reason i

to stop you from going down the drain!

For the past twenty years, baby boomers have slathered themselves in tons of lotions, creams, and oils in a vain attempt to stay young. These conditioners have entered the groundwater of the U.S.A., altering its chemical structure.

As a result, exposure to American water now causes Total Body Softening, or TBS.

S.O.S.

The first symptom occurs within ten minutes of immersion. This is *digitus prunus*, or "prune fingers." Unless contact is terminated, it is followed by *corpus prunus,* or "prune body."

The following time-lapse photography of TBS victim Omar Flitt shows the rapid progression of "prune body."

ONE HOUR	TWO HOURS	THREE HOURS

Flitt recovered from his three-hour bath, but not before being mistaken for dried fruit and served with cottage cheese to residents of the Kansas Home for the Kinda Tired.

While the body can rebound from pruniness, the brain has more difficulty with the softening effects of TBS. This can result in astonishing personality changes:

NFL quarterback Grit Mukkle took a five-hour soak.

•

He became the host of *Pinkies Out*, a TV show about gently drinking tea.

Controversial rap quartet Whaddup Widdat? took a six-hour bath.

•

They now perform on a popular preschool program.

Dictator Tito Kronk took a seven-hour dunk.

•

From the United Nations' time-out chair, he apologized for "starting wars and breaking stuff."

After eight hours of contact with conditioned water, bodily tissues relax so completely that it's possible to slip down the drain.

This happened to French diplomat Henri Ordure during a 1997 visit to Washington, D.C. Exhausted from using soap, Ordure fell asleep in the tub.

Twelve hours later, he awoke to find himself almost completely down the drain!

Fortunately, emergency plumbers were able to remove the pipe he was encased in. Unfortunately, they couldn't fix his posture.

There has been a vast improvement in TBS prevention since then. This is entirely due to *Drainwatch*, a spinoff from a popular TV show about lifeguards.

You see, Hollywood producers are the most at-risk group for Total Body Softening. Their demanding lives of parties and phone calls make it almost impossible for them to stay awake in the bath.

They overcame the problem by hiring the starlets and male models, rejected by the TV show, as drainguards. This idea spread throughout the country, saving lives and the careers of thousands of untalented actors.

DRAINWATCH

Dirk Croup guards the drain of the Nethery family in Ferfer, South Dakota. "It's tough to keep a tan," says Dirk, "but saving Mrs. Nethery from TBS makes it all worthwhile."

M. T. Noggin talks about saving teenager Matt Popover from going down the drain. "It's, like, a great job," enthuses M.T., "except, like, Matt is *always* going down the drain."

Do your bit to prevent Total Body Softening. Keep your tub time reasonable. And don't even try to take a bath at Matt Popover's house. The line of teenage boys goes around the block!

LOCATION: Big Bob's Bubble Gummery
Macon, Georgia

DATE & TIME: March 1, 2001
1:00 P.M.

LOG: Join production as gum wrapper. Disguise ineffective. (Note: Perhaps misunderstood "wrapper" concept.) Detected by Zsa-Zsa, the security poodle. Stuck to wall by staff. Loosen belt. Fall out of pants. Grab *GROWN-UP RULE #57* before chafing sets in.

TOP SECRET

CLASSIFIED
SECURITY
CLEARANCE A

GROWN-UP RULE #57:

Don't swallow your gum.

OFFICIAL REASON:

It gums up your insides.

THE TRUTH:

It doesn't gum up your insides. It coats them. And that's the problem. Without warning, you

inflate and float away!

The main ingredients of bubble gum are *resin* (sticky plant sap) and *latex* (stretchy plant sap). Once this coats your innards, you're just like a balloon. One big yawn or stifled sneeze and—*kafloot!*—you're ready for takeoff.

"But why," you may ask, "do grown-ups let us chew this stuff?" Half the answer is: Human beings have always chewed weird junk.

HISTORY OF GUM • PART 1

The ancient Greeks chewed gum made from mastic tree bark.

HISTORY OF GUM • PART 2

The Maya Indians chewed a rubbery tree juice called *chicle*.

HISTORY OF GUM • PART 3

New England colonists chewed the hardened sap of spruce trees.

The other half of the answer is: They don't know! Gum Inflation has been a military secret since it was discovered in Germany in 1905.

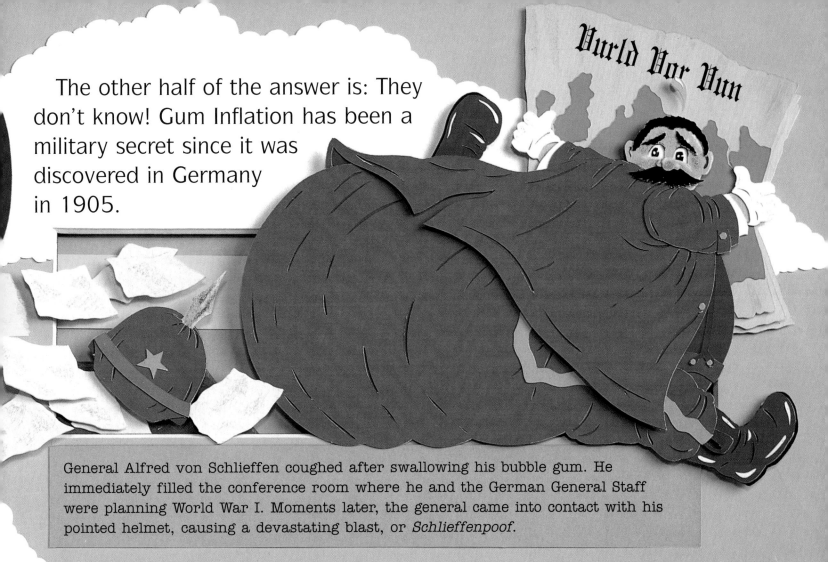

General Alfred von Schlieffen coughed after swallowing his bubble gum. He immediately filled the conference room where he and the German General Staff were planning World War I. Moments later, the general came into contact with his pointed helmet, causing a devastating blast, or *Schlieffenpoof*.

During the Cold War with the Soviet Union, the army tried to tame this amazing power. Brave volunteers swallowed their gum to develop a Floating Invasion Force that could enter enemy air space without detection. Unfortunately, these hardy GIs (code for *Gum Inside*) couldn't deflate without drawing attention to themselves.

FIF commander Colonel Elmo "Beans" Hartley grimaces as Private Larry "Toots" LaRue has a blowout at three thousand feet.

Instead of taking an unexpected flight, throw your gum in the trash. And if your dog gets hold of it, make sure he's on a long leash.

KNOWLEDGE OF GROWN-UPS

SECRET

UNBELIEVABLE!!! Stuck behind Grown-up Rule #57 was this fragment of Grown-up Rule #58! Using Brains, the head-filler used by nine out of ten secret agents, I have puzzled out the rest.

CLASSIFIED
SECURITY CLEARANCE **A**

RULE #58:

Don't stick your gum under the table.

OFFICIAL REASON:

It's disgusting.

TRUTH:

so folks don't get stuck!

Today's gum is so sticky that even a professional wrestler like Bruno "The Brute" Kelso cannot free himself. When ordinary people get stuck, they usually just give up and stay there—for *life*!

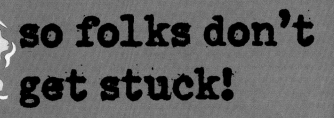

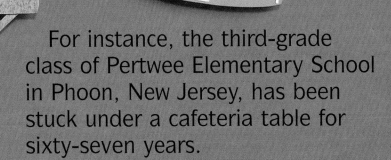

For instance, the third-grade class of Pertwee Elementary School in Phoon, New Jersey, has been stuck under a cafeteria table for sixty-seven years.

Again, dispose of your gum safely. And don't get it stuck in your hair—especially if you live near the airport!

LOCATION:
American Breakfast Council
Alexandria, Virginia

DATE & TIME: April 18, 2001
7:30 A.M.

LOG: Enter conference room as two eggs over easy with a side of bacon. Grab *GROWN-UP RULE #70* out of kitchen! Fling toast to prevent pursuit.

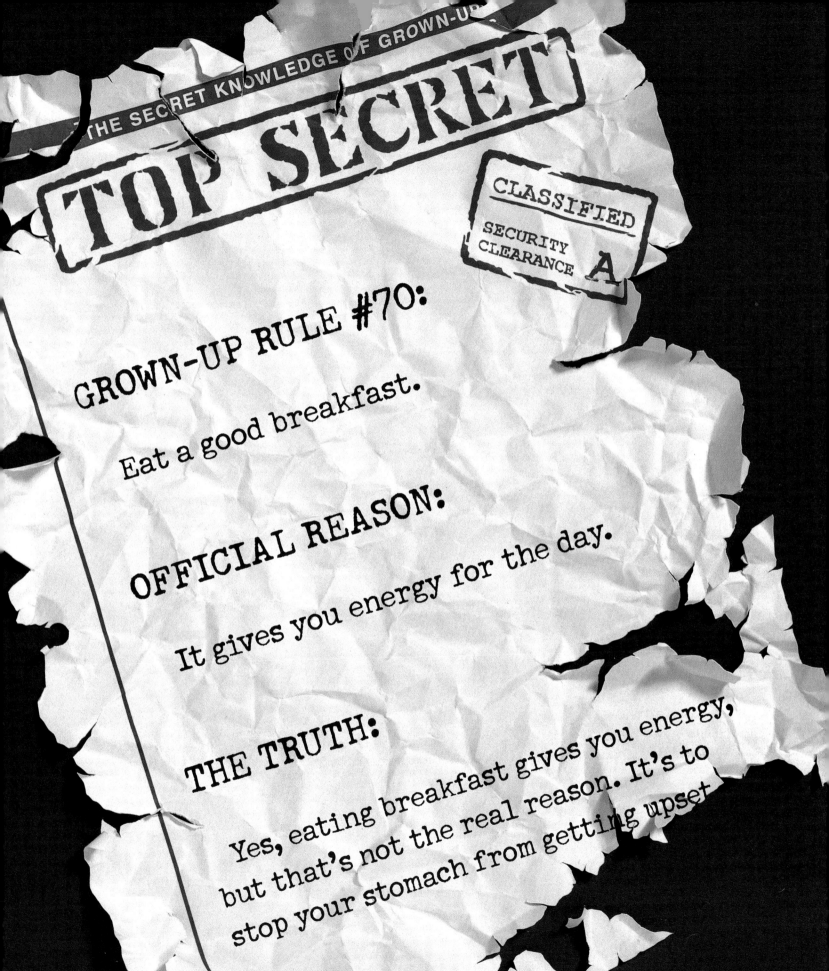

TOP SECRET

CLASSIFIED

SECURITY CLEARANCE A

GROWN-UP RULE #70:

Eat a good breakfast.

OFFICIAL REASON:

It gives you energy for the day.

THE TRUTH:

Yes, eating breakfast gives you energy, but that's not the real reason. It's to stop your stomach from getting upset

really upset!

Your stomach isn't just a little pink bag
that digests food. It's a somewhat surly organ
prone to mood swings. When it's full, it's happy.
When it's empty, it's not.

After a night without food, your stomach wakes up bad tempered.
(Why else would it growl?) When it doesn't get breakfast, it throws a
tantrum. It runs around your insides kicking the wall and pinching
better-behaved organs. If food still doesn't arrive, the stomach takes
over your central nervous system.

Contrary to popular belief, the central nervous system is not a web
of neurons, morons, and croutons. It's just a steering wheel, gas pedal,
brake, and gear shift. The stomach shoves the driver (usually the
spleen) out of the seat and attempts to guide the body toward a
food source.

Driving blindly, the stomach always oversteers. The resulting turns cause varying degrees of distress.

But what's worse is unwinding. This happens when the stomach lets go of the wheel to grab breakfast. Unwinding from 1,440 degrees isn't so bad. It only causes uncontrollable face slapping. Unwinding from 2,880 degrees, however, can knock out a moose!

90-DEGREE TURN:	180-DEGREE TURN:	360-DEGREE TURN:
Must walk sideways.	Must walk backwards.	Walking okay, but belly button creased.

Some people have turned their spinning into new careers of salad drying and tunnel drilling, but most folks find it really annoying. So, unless you enjoy being dizzy, eat your breakfast!

LOCATION:
Orville's TV & VCR Repair
Vapors, Vermont

DATE & TIME: June 28, 2001
2:15 P.M.

LOG: Penetrate facility as old television set. Snatch *GROWN-UP RULE #87* off worktable! Taken into back room to have cable installed! Break free. Exit as happy, square-headed customer.

TOP SECRET

CLASSIFIED
SECURITY
CLEARANCE **A**

GROWN-UP RULE #87:

Don't watch TV late at night.

OFFICIAL REASONS:

It will strain your eyes.
You'll be tired the next day.

THE TRUTH:

Both these reasons sound very reasonable, but they're not true. The real reason is

so the actors can take a break!

Since the 1950s, people have been told that TV shows are "broadcast" by "electronic waves" through "the air" and picked up by your TV set's "antenna." And now they tell us it's done with "cable" and "satellite dish." Ridiculous!

Your television is filled with tiny actors. Every TV has a highly trained cast that performs shows, commercials, news, and sports. This shocking truth isn't so surprising when you consider the real history of television.

It didn't start in the 1920s. It began with the Dawn of Humanity with the Neanderthal Broadcasting Company (NBC).

There was only one channel (Ogg), and programs were limited to cooking shows and banging two rocks together.

About the time fire was invented, the Cro-Magnon Broadcasting System (CBS) arrived.

Neanderthals enjoy *Cooking with Naargh!* on their newly carved TV.

Cro-Magnons giggle at *Ungak Ooglik* ("Wheel of Misfortune") on their overheated straw TV.

TVs were fashioned of thatch and twine. There were now two channels (Ogg and Bluk). Programs included game shows and newscasts of TVs burning up.

The Ancient Broadcasting Company (ABC) modernized these prehistoric networks. It allowed commercials for corn, wheat, busted chariots, and used arks. More important, it hired actors.

Eventually, audiences grew tired of only one or two actors stuffed in their TVs.

They wanted variety. In response, actors got smaller so more of them could cram into shows. Today, with television on all the time, actors are teensy-weensy. So give them a break. Go to bed at a decent time and let them stretch their legs!